Behold the **scorpion** STINGALING,
a most **repulsive** ugly thing!

al is half so VILE

as

ile.

Roy, a plump

half

led,

bu

poiled.

ked book

VORST...

ROALD DAHL was a spy, ace fighter pilot, chocolate historian and medical inventor. He was also the author of *Charlie and the Chocolate Factory*, *Matilda*, *The BFG* and many more brilliant stories. He remains THE WORLD'S NUMBER ONE STORYTELLER.

QUENTIN BLAKE has illustrated more than three hundred books and was Roald Dahl's favourite illustrator. In 1980 he won the prestigious Kate Greenaway Medal. In 1999 he became the first ever Children's Laureate and in 2013 he was knighted for services to illustration.

ROALD DAHL

DIRTY BEASTS

Illustrated by Quentin Blake

PUFFIN

~ To Alfhild, Else and Asta ~

Find out more about Roald Dahl
by visiting the website at
www.roalddahl.com

PUFFIN BOOKS

UK | USA | Canada | Ireland | Australia | India | New Zealand | South Africa

Puffin Books is part of the Penguin Random House group of companies
whose addresses can be found at global.penguinrandomhouse.com.

www.penguin.co.uk   www.puffin.co.uk   www.ladybird.co.uk

 Penguin
Random House
UK

Text first published in the USA by Farrar, Straus and Giroux 1983
This edition first published in Great Britain by Jonathan Cape 1984
Published by Puffin Books 1986
This edition published 2016
003

Text copyright © Roald Dahl Nominee Ltd, 1983
Illustrations copyright © Quentin Blake, 1984
The moral right of Roald Dahl and Quentin Blake has been asserted
A CIP catalogue record for this book is available from the British Library
Printed in China

ISBN: 978−0−141−36933−4

All correspondence to:
Puffin Books, Penguin Random House Children's, 80 Strand, London WC2R 0RL

The Pig

In England once there lived a big
And wonderfully clever pig.
To everybody it was plain
That Piggy had a massive brain.
He worked out sums inside his head,
There was no book he hadn't read,
He knew what made an airplane fly,
He knew how engines worked and why.
He knew all this, but in the end
One question drove him round the bend:
He simply couldn't puzzle out
What LIFE was really all about.
What was the reason for his birth?
Why was he placed upon this earth?
His giant brain went round and round.
Alas, no answer could be found,
Till suddenly one wondrous night,
All in a flash, he saw the light.
He jumped up like a ballet dancer
And yelled, "By gum, I've got the answer!"

"They want my bacon slice by slice
"To sell at a tremendous price!
"They want my tender juicy chops
"To put in all the butchers' shops!
"They want my pork to make a roast
"And that's the part'll cost the most!
"They want my sausages in strings!
"They even want my chitterlings!
"The butcher's shop! The carving knife!
"That is the reason for my life!"
Such thoughts as these are not designed
To give a pig great peace of mind.

Next morning, in comes Farmer Bland,
A pail of pigswill in his hand,
And Piggy with a mighty roar,
Bashes the farmer to the floor . . .
Now comes the rather grizzly bit
So let's not make too much of it,
Except that you *must* understand
That Piggy *did eat* Farmer Bland,
He ate him up from head to toe,
Chewing the pieces nice and slow.
It took an hour to reach the feet,
Because there was so much to eat,
And when he'd finished, Pig, of course,
Felt absolutely no remorse.
Slowly he scratched his brainy head
And with a little smile, he said,
"I had a fairly powerful hunch
"That he might have me for his lunch.
"And so, because I feared the worst,
"I thought I'd better eat *him* first."

The Crocodile

No animal is half so vile
As Crocky-Wock the crocodile.
On Saturdays he likes to crunch
Six juicy children for his lunch,
And he especially enjoys
Just three of each, three girls, three boys.
He smears the boys (to make them hot)
With mustard from the mustard pot.

But mustard doesn't go with girls,
It tastes all wrong with plaits and curls.
With them, what goes extremely well
Is butterscotch and caramel.
It's such a super marvellous treat
When boys are hot and girls are sweet.
At least that's Crocky's point of view.
He ought to know. He's had a few.

That's all for now. It's time for bed
Lie down and rest your sleepy head . . .
Ssh! *Listen!* What is that I hear
Gallumphing softly up the stair?
Go lock the door and fetch my gun!
Go on, child, hurry! Quickly, run!
No, stop! Stand back! He's coming in!
Oh, look, that greasy greenish skin!
The shining teeth, the greedy smile!
It's CROCKY-WOCK, THE CROCODILE!

The Lion

The lion just adores to eat
A lot of red and tender meat,
And if you ask the lion what
Is much the tenderest of the lot,
He will not say a roast of lamb
Or curried beef or devilled ham
Or crispy pork or corned beef hash
Or sausages or mutton mash.
Then could it be a big plump hen?
He answers no. What is it, then?
Oh, lion dear, could I not make
You happy with a lovely steak?
Could I entice you from your lair
With rabbit-pie or roasted hare?
The lion smiled and shook his head.
He came up very close and said,
"The meat I am about to chew
Is neither steak nor chops. IT'S YOU."

The Scorpion

You ought to thank your lucky star
   That here in England where you are
You'll never find (or so it's said)
A scorpion inside your bed.
The scorpion's name is Stingaling,
A most repulsive ugly thing,
And I would never recommend
That you should treat him as a friend.
His scaly skin is black as black
With armour-plate upon his back.
Observe his scowling murderous face,
His wicked eyes, his lack of grace,
Note well his long and crinkly tail.
And when it starts to swish and flail,
Oh gosh! Watch out! Jump back, I say,
And run till you're a mile away.
The moment that his tail goes *swish*
He has but one determined wish,
He wants to make a sudden jump
And sting you hard upon your rump.

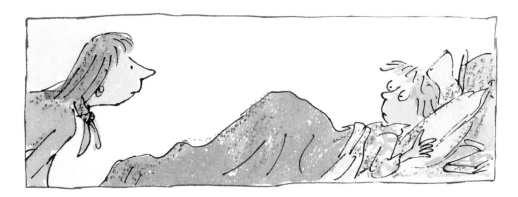

"What *is* the matter, darling child?
"Why do you look so tense and wild?"
"Oh mummy, underneath the sheet
"There's something moving on my feet,
"Some horrid creepy crawly thing,
"D'you think it could be Stingaling?"
"What nonsense child! You're teasing me."
"I'm not, I'm not! It's reached my knee!
"It's going . . . going up my thigh!
"Oh mummy, catch it quickly! Try!
"It's on . . . it's on my bottom now!
"It's . . . *Ow! Ow-ow! Ow-ow! OW-OW!*"

The Ant-Eater

Some wealthy folks from U.S.A.,
   Who lived near San Francisco Bay,
Possessed an only child called Roy,
A plump and unattractive boy –
Half-baked, half-witted and half-boiled,
But worst of all, most dreadfully spoiled.
Whatever Roy desired each day,
His father bought him right away –
Toy motor-cars, electric trains,
The latest model aeroplanes,
A colour television-set,
A saxophone, a clarinet,
Expensive teddy-bears that talked,
And animals that walked and squawked.
That house contained sufficient toys
To thrill a half a million boys.
(As well as this, young Roy would choose,
Two pairs a week of brand-new shoes.)
And now he stood there shouting, "What
"On earth is there I haven't got?
"How hard to think of something new!
"The choices are extremely few!"

Then added, as he scratched his ear,
"Hold it! I've got a good idea!
"I think the next thing I must get
"Should be a most peculiar pet –
"The kind that no one else has got –
"A giant ANT-EATER! Why not?"
As soon as father heard the news,
He quickly wrote to all the zoos.
"Dear Sirs," he said, "My dear keepers,
"Do any of you have ant-eaters?"
They answered by return of mail.
"Our ant-eaters are not for sale."
Undaunted, Roy's fond parent hurled
More messages across the world.
He said, "I'll pay you through the nose
"If you can get me one of those."
At last he found an Indian gent
(He lived near Delhi, in a tent),
Who said that he would sacrifice
His pet for an enormous price
(The price demanded, if you please,
Was fifty thousand gold rupees).
The ant-eater arrived half-dead.
It looked at Roy and softly said,
"I'm famished. Do you think you could
"Please give me just a little food?
"A crust of bread, a bit of meat?
"I haven't had a thing to eat
"In all the time I was at sea,
"For nobody looked after me."
Roy shouted, "No! No bread or meat!
"Go find some ants! They're what you eat!"
The starving creature crawled away.
It searched the garden night and day,
It hunted every inch of ground,
But not one single ant it found.

"Please give me food!" the creature cried.
"Go find an ant!" the boy replied.

By chance, upon that very day,
Roy's father's sister came to stay –
A foul old hag of eighty-three
Whose name, it seems, was Dorothy.
She said to Roy, "Come let us sit
"Out in the sun and talk a bit."
Roy said, "I don't believe you've met
"My new and most unusual pet?"
He pointed down among the stones
Where something lay, all skin and bones.
"Ant-eater!" he yelled. "Don't lie there yawning!
    "This is my ant! Come say good morning!"
        (Some people in the U.S.A.
            Have trouble with the words they say.
            However hard they try, they can't
            Pronounce a simple word like AUNT.
        Instead of AUNT, they call it ANT,
    Instead of CAN'T, they call it KANT.)
        Roy yelled, "Come here, you so-and-so!
        "My ant would like to say hello!"
    Slowly, the creature raised its head.
        "D'you mean that that's an *ant?*" it said.
        "Of course!" cried Roy. "Ant Dorothy!
        "This ant is over eighty-three."
        The creature smiled. Its tummy rumbled.
        It licked its starving lips and mumbled,
        "A giant ant! By gosh, a winner!
        "At last I'll get a decent dinner!
        "No matter if it's eighty-three.
        "If that's an ant, then it's for me!"
Then, taking very careful aim,
It pounced upon the startled dame.
It grabbed her firmly by the hair
And ate her up right then and there,
Murmuring as it chewed the feet,
"The largest ant I'll ever eat."

Meanwhile, our hero Roy had sped
In terror to the potting-shed,
And tried to make himself obscure
Behind a pile of horse-manure.
But ant-eater came sneaking in
(Already it was much less thin)
And said to Roy, "You little squirt,
"I think I'll have you for dessert."

The Porcupine

Each Saturday I shout "Hooray!"
For that's my pocket-money day,
(Although it's clearly understood
I only get it when I'm good.)
This week my parents had been told
That I had been as good as gold,
So after breakfast 50p
My generous father gave to me.
Like lightning down the road I ran
Until I reached the sweet-shop man,
And bought the chocolates of my dreams,
A great big bag of raspberry creams.
There is a secret place I know
Where I quite often like to go,
Beyond the wood, behind some rocks,
A super place for guzzling chocs.
When I arrived, I quickly found
A comfy-looking little mound,
Quite clean and round and earthy-brown
Just right, I thought, for sitting down.
Here I will sit all morning long
And eat until my chocs are gone.
I sat. I screamed. I jumped a foot!
Would you believe that I had put
That tender little rump of mine
Upon a giant porcupine!
My backside seemed to catch on fire!
A hundred red-hot bits of wire
A hundred prickles sticking in
And puncturing my precious skin!
I ran for home. I shouted, "Mum!
"Behold the prickles in my bum!"
My mum, who always keeps her head,
Bent down to look and then she said,

"I personally am not about
"To try to pull *those* prickles out.
"I think a job like this requires
"The services of Mr Myers."
I shouted, "Not the dentist! No!
"Oh mum, why don't *you* have a go?"
I begged her twice, I begged her thrice,
But grown-ups never take advice.
She said, "A dentist's very strong.
"He pulls things out the whole day long."
She drove me quickly into town,
And then they turned me upside down
Upon the awful dentist's chair,
While two strong nurses held me there.

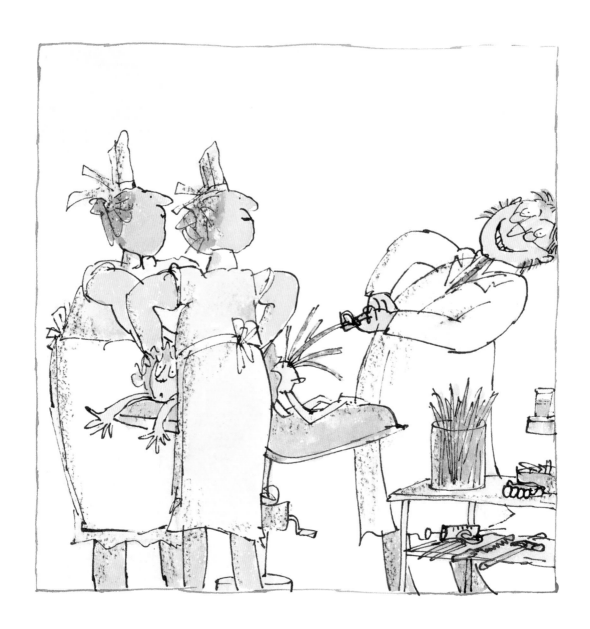

Enter the dreaded Mr Myers
Waving a massive pair of pliers.
"This is," he cried with obvious glee,
"A new experience for me.
"Quite honestly I can't pretend
"I've ever pulled things from *this* end."
He started pulling one by one
And yelling "My, oh my, what fun!"

I shouted "Help!" I shouted "Ow!"
He said, "It's nearly over now.
"For heaven's sake, don't squirm about!
"Here goes! The last one's coming out!"
The dentist pulled and out it came,
And then I heard the man exclaim,
"Let us now talk about the fees.
"That will be fifty guineas, please."
My mother is a gutsy bird
And never one to mince a word.
She cried, "By gosh, that's jolly steep!"
He answered, "No, it's very cheap.
"My dear woman, can't you see
"That if it hadn't been for me
"This child could go another year
"With prickles sticking in her rear."
So that was that. Oh, what a day!
And what a fuss! But by the way,
I think I know why porcupines
Surround themselves with prickly spines.
It is to stop some silly clown
From squashing them by sitting down.
Don't copy me. Don't be a twit.
Be sure you LOOK before you SIT.

The Cow

Please listen while I tell you now
About a most fantastic cow.
Miss Milky Daisy was her name,
And when, aged seven months, she came
To live with us, she did her best
To look the same as all the rest.
But Daisy, as we all could see
Had some kind of deformity,
A funny sort of bumpy lump
On either side, above the rump.
Now, not so very long ago,
These bumpy lumps began to grow,
And three or maybe four months later,
(I stood there, an enthralled spectator)
These bumpy lumps burst wide apart
And out there came (I cross my heart)
Of all the wondrous marvellous things,
A pair of gold and silver wings!
A cow with wings! A flying cow!
I'd never seen one up to now.
"Oh Daisy dear, can this be true?"
She flapped her wings and up she flew!
Most gracefully she climbed up high,
She fairly whizzed across the sky.
You should have seen her dive and swoop!
She even did a loop the loop!
Of course, almost immediately
Her picture was on live T.V.,
And millions came each day to stare
At Milky Daisy in the air.
They shouted "Jeepers Creepers! Wow!
"It really is a flying cow!"
They laughed and clapped and cheered and waved,
And all of them were well-behaved

Except for one quite horrid man
Who'd travelled from Afghanistan.
This fellow, standing in the crowd,
Raised up his voice and yelled aloud,
"That silly cow! Hey, listen Daisy!
"I think you're absolutely crazy!"
Unfortunately Daisy heard
Quite clearly every single word.
"By gosh," she cried, "what awful cheek!
"Who is this silly foreign freak?"
She dived, and using all her power
She got to sixty miles an hour.
"Bombs gone!" she cried. "Take that!" she said,
And dropped a cowpat on his head.

The Toad and the Snail

I really am most awfully fond
  Of playing in the lily-pond.
I take off shoes and socks and coat
And paddle with my little boat.
Now yesterday, quite suddenly,
A giant toad came up to me.
This toad was easily as big
As any fair-sized fattish pig.
He smiled and said "How do you do?
"Hello! Good morning! How are you?"

(His face somehow reminded me
Of mummy's sister Emily.)
The toad said, "Don't you think I'm fine?
"Admire these lovely legs of mine,
"And I am sure you've never seen
"A toad so gloriously green!"
I said, "So far as I can see,
"You look just like Aunt Emily."
He said, "I'll bet Aunt Emily
"Can't jump one half as high as me.
"Hop on my back, young friend," he cried,
"I'll take you for a marvellous ride."
As I got on, I thought, oh blimey,
Oh, deary me. How wet and slimy!
"Sit further back," he said. "That's right.
"I'm going to jump, so hold on tight."
He jumped! Oh, how he jumped! By gum,
I thought my final hour had come!
My wretched eardrums popped and fizzed.
My eyeballs watered. Up we whizzed.
I clung on tight. I shouted, "How
"Much further are we going now?"
Toad said, his face all wreathed in smiles,
"With every jump, it's fifty miles!"
Quite literally, we jumped all over,

From Scotland to The Cliffs of Dover!
Above the Cliffs, we stopped for tea,
And Toad said, gazing at the sea,
"What do you say we take a chance,
"And jump from England into France?"
I said, "Oh dear, d'you think we oughta?
"I'd hate to finish in the water."
But toads, you'll find, don't give a wink
For what we little children think.
He didn't bother to reply.
He jumped! You should have seen us fly!
We simply soared across the sea,
The marvellous Mister Toad and me.

Then down we came, and down and down,
And landed in a funny town.
We landed hard, in fact we bounced.
"We're there! It's France!" the Toad announced.
He said, "You must admit it's grand
"To jump into a foreign land.
"No boats, no bicycles, no trains,
"No cars, no noisy aeroplanes."
Just then, we heard a fearful shout,
"Oh, heavens above!" the Toad cried out.
I turned and saw a frightening sight –
On every side, to left, to right,
People were running down the road,
Running at me and Mister Toad,
And every person, man and wife
Was brandishing a carving-knife.
It didn't take me very long
To figure there was something wrong.
And yet, how could a small boy know,
For nobody had told me so,
That Frenchmen aren't like you or me,
They do things very differently.
They won't say "yards", they call them "metres",

And they're the *most peculiar* eaters:
A Frenchman frequently regales
Himself with half-a-dozen SNAILS!
The greedy ones will gulp a score
Of these foul brutes and ask for more.
(In many of the best hotels
The people also eat the shells.)
Imagine that! My stomach turns!
One might as well eat slugs or worms!
But wait. Read on a little bit.
You haven't heard the half of it.

These French go even more agog
If someone offers them a FROG!
(You'd better fetch a basin quick
In case you're going to be sick.)
The bits of frog they like to eat
Are thighs and calves and toes and feet.
The French will gobble loads and loads
Of legs they chop off frogs and toads.

They think it's absolutely ripping
To guzzle frogs-legs fried in dripping.
That's why the whole town and their wives
Were rushing us with carving-knives.
They screamed in French, "Well I'll be blowed!
"What legs there are upon that toad!
"Chop them! Skin them! Cook them! Fry them!
"All of us are going to try them!"
"Toad!" I cried. "I'm not a funk,
"But ought we not to do a bunk?
"These rascals haven't come to greet you.
"All they want to do is eat you!"

Toad turned his head and looked at me,
And said, as cool as cool could be,
"Calm down and listen carefully please,
"I often come to France to tease
"These crazy French who long to eat
"My lovely tender froggy meat.
"I am a MAGIC TOAD!" he cried.
"And I don't ever have to hide!
"Stay where you are! Don't move!" he said,
And pressed a button on his head.
At once, there came a blinding flash,
And then the most almighty crash,
And sparks were bursting all around,
And smoke was rising from the ground . . .
When all the smoke had cleared away
The Frenchmen with their knives cried, "*Hey!*
"Where is the toad? Where has he gone?"
You see, I now was sitting on
A wonderfully ENORMOUS SNAIL!
His shell was smooth and brown and pale,
And I was so high off the ground
That I could see for miles around.
The Snail said, "Hello! Greetings! Hail!
"I was a Toad. Now I'm a Snail.
"I had to change the way I looked
"To save myself from being cooked."
"Oh Snail," I said, "I'm not so sure.
"I think they're starting up once more."
The French were shouting, "What a snail!
"Oh, what a monster! What a whale!
"He makes the toad look titchy small!
"There's lovely snail-meat for us all!
"We'll bake the creature in his shell
"And ring aloud the dinner-bell!
"Get garlic, parsley, butter, spices!
"We'll cut him into fifty slices!

"Come sharpen up your carving-knives!
"This is the banquet of our lives!"
I murmured through my quivering lips,
"Oh Snail, I think we've had our chips."
The Snail replied, "I disagree.
"Those greedy French, they'll not eat me."
But on they came. They screamed, "Yahoo!
"Surround the brute and run him through!"
Good gracious, I could almost feel
The pointed blades, the shining steel!
But Snail was cool as cool could be.
He turned his head and winked at me,
And murmured, "Au revoir, farewell,"
And pulled a lever on his shell.
I looked around. The Snail had gone!
And *now* who was I sitting on? . . .
Oh what relief! What joy! Because
At last I'd found a friend. It was
The gorgeous, glamorous, absurd,
Enchanting ROLY-POLY BIRD!
He turned and whispered in my ear,
"Well, fancy seeing you, my dear!"
Then up he went in glorious flight.
I clutched his neck and hung on tight.

We fairly raced across the sky,
The Roly-Poly Bird and I,
And landed safely just beyond
The fringes of the lily-pond.
When I got home I never told
A solitary single soul
What I had done or where I'd been
Or any of the things I'd seen.
I did not even say I rode
Upon a giant jumping toad,
'Cause if I had, I knew that they
Would not believe me anyway.
But you and I know well it's true.
We know I jumped, we know I flew.
We're sure it all took place, although
Not one of us will ever know,
We'll never, never understand
Why children go to Wonderland.

The Tummy Beast

One afternoon I said to mummy,
   "Who is this person in my tummy?
"He must be small and very thin
"Or how could he have gotten in?"
My mother said from where she sat,
"It isn't nice to talk like that."
"It's true!" I cried. "I swear it, mummy!
"There *is* a person in my tummy!
"He talks to me at night in bed,
"He's always asking to be fed,
"Throughout the day, he screams at me,
"Demanding sugar buns for tea.
"He tells me it is not a sin
"To go and raid the biscuit tin.
"I know quite well it's awfully wrong
"To guzzle food the whole day long,
"But really I can't help it, mummy,
"Not with this person in my tummy."
"You horrid child!" my mother cried.
"Admit it right away, you've lied!
"You're simply trying to produce
"A silly asinine excuse!
"*You* are the greedy guzzling brat!
"And that is why you're always fat!"
I tried once more, "*Believe me*, mummy,
"There is a person in my tummy."
"I've had enough!" my mother said,
"You'd better go at once to bed!"

Just then, a nicely timed event
Delivered me from punishment.
Deep in my tummy something stirred,
And then an awful noise was heard,
A snorting grumbling grunting sound
That made my tummy jump around.
My darling mother nearly died,

"My goodness, what was that?" she cried.
At once, the tummy voice came through,
It shouted, "Hey there! Listen you!
"I'm getting hungry! I want eats!
"I want lots of chocs and sweets!
"Get me half a pound of nuts!
"Look snappy or I'll twist your guts!"
"*That's him!*" I cried. "*He's in my tummy!*
"So now do you believe me, mummy?"

But mummy answered nothing more,
For she had fainted on the floor.

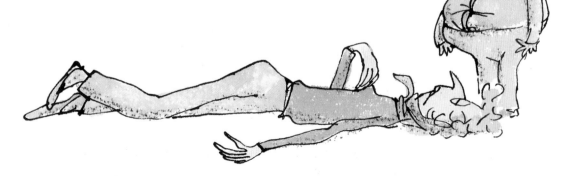

STORIES ARE GOOD FOR YOU.

Roald Dahl said,
*'If you have good thoughts, they will shine
out of your face like sunbeams and you
will always look lovely.'*

We believe in doing good things.
That's why ten per cent of all Roald Dahl income*
goes to our charity partners. We have supported
causes including: specialist children's nurses, grants for
families in need, and educational outreach programmes.
Thank you for helping us to sustain this vital work.

Find out more at roalddahl.com

HOW MANY HAVE YOU READ?

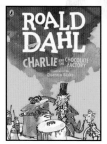   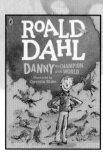 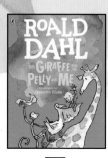 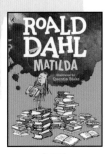

☐ ☐ ☐ ☐ ☐ ☐

 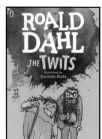   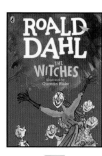 

☐ ☐ ☐ ☐ ☐ ☐

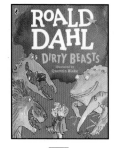    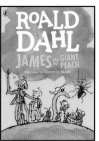

☐ ☐ ☐ ☐ ☐

FEWER THAN 5? WHOOPSY-SPLUNKERS! You've got some reading to do!

BETWEEN 5 AND 10? Wonderful surprises await! Keep reading . . .

MORE THAN 10? Whoopee! Which was your favourite?